This Little Tiger book belongs to:

_____

_____

_____

To Avery, who would most probably
cuddle a crocodile too! - S S

To Madeleine, my sweet little hungry crocodile - J D

LITTLE TIGER PRESS LTD,
an imprint of the Little Tiger Group
1 Coda Studios, 189 Munster Road, London SW6 6AW
www.littletiger.co.uk

First published in Spain 2020
This edition published in Great Britain 2022

Text copyright © Steve Smallman 2020
Illustrations copyright © Joëlle Dreidemy 2020
Steve Smallman and Joëlle Dreidemy have asserted their rights to be identified as the
author and illustrator of this work under the Copyright, Designs and Patents Act, 1988
A CIP catalogue record for this book is available from the British Library

Printed in China · LTP/2800/3494/1020
10 9 8 7 6 5 4 3 2 1

# THE CROCODILE WHO CAME FOR DINNER

STEVE SMALLMAN · JOËLLE DREIDEMY

LITTLE TIGER
LONDON

Hotpot was a lamb, and Wolf was a wolf.
And they were the very best of friends.
Sometimes they did lamby things
like skipping through meadows.
And sometimes they did wolfy
things like howling at the moon.

AROOO

BAAAA-

Then, one night, they
spotted an egg.
A big egg!

"Ooh, lovely!" cried Wolf. "I can
make an omelette!"
Hotpot gave Wolf a hard stare.
"No, Woof, not omelette, baby bird."

Hotpot made Wolf check
all the nests nearby, but
nobody had lost an egg.

"What do you do with a lost egg?" wondered Wolf.
"Not 'lost', Woof," whispered Hotpot. "Found!"
Then she wrapped the egg up warmly and
carried it carefully home.

"You can live with us!" Hotpot told the egg. Wolf nodded and was trying not to think of how delicious an omelette would be when . . .

CRACK

went the egg.

And out popped a little crocodile!

Hello, Omelette!

Omelette climbed onto
Wolf's shoulder and
nibbled his ear.
   "He's hungry!"
laughed Hotpot.
   "But what do crocodiles
eat?" wondered Wolf.

Ouch!

They soon found out that
crocodiles eat everything.
Even wolf tails!

It was getting late, so Wolf tucked Hotpot into bed and fetched a blanket for Omelette.

But the crocodile had already settled down . . . on Wolf's bed!

"I'm not sure," yawned Wolf, sinking into his chair, "that snuggling up with a nippy-toothed crocodile is a good idea!"

Then Omelette scrambled up and snuggled against Wolf's chest.

And Wolf, who had never been cuddled by an Omelette before, thought that maybe everything would be okay.

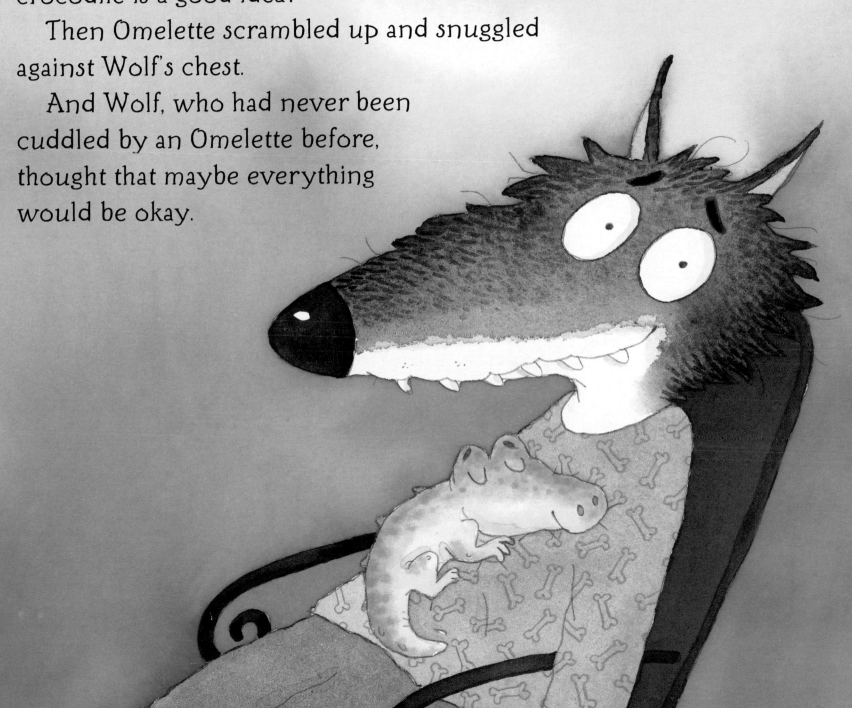

But in the morning . . .
   "What happened to my kitchen?" cried Wolf.
   "Omelette happened!" said Hotpot.
   "We'd better take him out for a walk," sighed
Wolf, "before he makes any more mess!"

Omelette burst out of the front door just as Wolf's friends arrived.

"Eeeeek! A crocodile!" they wailed as Omelette leapt up . . .

He'll gobble us up!

. . . and gave them all a big, slobbery kiss!

Well that was a surprise!

What a lovely little fella!

I knew he wouldn't hurt us!

Wolf and Hotpot chased Omelette through the trees . . .

SPLASH!

. . . where Omelette dived in for a swim.
"He'll gobble us up!" cried a bunny.
"Omelette wouldn't hurt a fly!" called Wolf.
"He's only little."

"He is now," grumbled
Badger. "But not for long!"

Badger was right.
Omelette grew and grew!

But although he was noisy,
and messy, and nibbly, Wolf
and Hotpot loved him.
And Omelette loved
them right back.

Pretty soon everyone in the wood loved Omelette. Well, nearly everyone.

"You won't be laughing when that crocodile gobbles you up!" warned Badger, as black rain clouds darkened the forest. That night there was a terrible storm.

And in the morning the forest
was flooded.

"Omelette's missing!" cried Hotpot.
They rushed out to look for him.

Mummy Duck shouted to them from the riverbank.

"Help! My ducklings! They're being swept away!"

"Who will save them?" wailed the woodland animals.
"Omelette!" cried Hotpot, pointing at the crocodile
swimming bravely towards the ducklings.
Then everyone GASPED as Omelette opened
his mouth and . . .

He's going to
rescue them!

He's nearly
got them!

"He gobbled them up!" shrieked the rabbits.

"I told you this would happen!" bellowed Badger.

Omelette trotted up to the animals who shrank back in fright.

He opened his mouth . . .

. . . and out jumped one, two, three
little ducklings.
   "Well done, Omelette!" cheered Wolf,
and Hotpot gave him a great big hug.

"HOORAY FOR OMELETTE!" everyone cheered.

"Well, it's like I've always said," blustered Badger, "it's very useful to have a crocodile around."

Hotpot gave Badger a hard stare and Badger stopped talking. Then Wolf took Hotpot and Omelette home, where they all lived snappily ever after.

# More terrific tales

## from Steve Smallman!

POO IN THE ZOO
Steve Smallman ~ Ada Grey

POO IN THE ZOO
THE GREAT POO MYSTERY
Steve Smallman
Ada Grey

ITCHY SCRITCHY SCRATCHY PANTS
Steve Smallman
Elina Ellis

Bear's BIG Bottom
STEVE SMALLMAN & EMMA YARLETT

I'M NOT GRUMPY!
steve SMALLMAN
caroline PEDLER

Scaredy BEAR
Steve Smallman
Caroline Pedler

For information regarding any of the above titles or for our catalogue, please contact us: Little Tiger Press Ltd, 1 Coda Studios, 189 Munster Road, London SW6 6AW · Tel: 020 7385 6333
E-mail: contact@littletiger.co.uk · www.littletiger.co.uk